Pet Friends Forever

Mice Capades

by Diana G. Gallagher

illustrated by Adriana Isabel Juárez Puglisi

Raintree is an imprint of Capstone Global Library Limited,
a company incorporated in England and Wales having its registered office at 7 Pilgrim
Street, London, EC4V 6LB – Registered company number: 6695582

www.raintreepublishers.co.uk
myorders@raintreepublishers.co.uk

Edited by Helen Cox Cannons
Designed by Kristi Carlson and Philippa Jenkins
Original illustrations © Capstone Global Library Ltd 2014
Image Credits: Shutterstock/Kudryashka (pattern)

Originated by Capstone Global Library Ltd
Production by Helen McCreath
Printed and bound in China

ISBN 978 1 406 27967 2
18 17 16 15 14
10 9 8 7 6 5 4 3 2 1

British Library Cataloguing in Publication Data
A full catalogue record for this book is available from the British Library.

TABLE OF CONTENTS

1

Who wants to be a mad scientist?

On Wednesday afternoon, Mrs Lockwood made an important announcement to her Year 5 class.

"Clark Primary School will be hosting a science fair next week," she told them. "Everyone is expected to participate. You'll each be doing a project and giving a presentation to the class."

Some of the children groaned, but Kyle Blake and Mia Perez grinned at each other in excitement. This assignment was perfect for them. Kyle and Mia were next-door neighbours and best friends. More importantly, they both loved animals and science. Mostly because they wanted to be veterinarians like Kyle's mum, Dr Blake, when they grew up.

Billy Evans raised his hand. "Can I make stink bombs?" he asked.

"Eww!" Lucy Owens squealed.

"Do you have a scientific question about stink bombs, Billy?" Mrs Lockwood asked. She wasn't annoyed or disgusted.

Billy shrugged. "No, I just want to make stink bombs," he said.

Mia rolled her eyes. Billy always wanted to do the grossest thing possible.

Mrs Lockwood smiled. "Well, stink bombs could be a project for the science fair," she said. "But your project has to follow these steps." She passed out an instruction sheet to all the pupils.

There were six steps written on the front of the handout.

1) Ask a question.

2) Find out what is already known.

3) Decide what you think the answer will be.

4) Experiment to test your hypothesis.

5) Record what happens.

6) Draw a conclusion: Was your hypothesis right or wrong?

"I need to know what your projects will be by tomorrow," Mrs Lockwood continued. "If you don't have an idea, there are some ideas for projects listed on the back of your instruction sheet."

One of the pupils raised his hand. "What if my mum or dad wants to help?" he asked.

"Parents can help build anything that requires using power tools," Mrs Lockwood said. "But you have to do the research and experiment on your own."

Mia leaned over to Kyle's desk. "Are you going to do a project about animals?" she whispered.

Kyle shook his head. "I don't think so," he said.

Mia looked surprised. "Why not? You know a lot about them."

"That's exactly why," Kyle said. "It will be more fun to do something else."

"Do you have any ideas?" Mia asked.

Kyle nodded. "I like baseball, but I'm not a very good hitter," he admitted. "I thought that using a different bat could help. I think I'll do an experiment to find out if using a metal bat or a wooden bat makes a difference."

"That's a cool experiment," Mia said.

"Thanks," Kyle said. "What about you?"

"I don't know yet," Mia said. "I like to help my mum in the garden, so maybe something with plants."

"Good idea," Kyle said.

When the bell rang, Ryan Murray stopped Kyle and Mia by the door. "You know a lot about animals, right?" he asked them.

"Yeah," Kyle said. "My mum is a vet. Why?"

"I want to do my experiment with mice," Ryan explained. "I want to find out if music makes them cleverer. But I don't really know anything about mice. So I might need some advice."

"No problem," Kyle said. "Mia and I will be happy to help."

2

Beg, borrow and buy

The next afternoon, Kyle and Mia met
Ryan. Their plan was to head to Mr J's Pet
Haven so they could look at some mice. Mr
J's Pet Haven was the best pet shop in town.
Mr Jabowski, who everyone called Mr J, had
opened it thirty years ago. His shop didn't have
as much stuff as some of the big chain stores,
but he always remembered his customers and
their pets.

"Mr J is really nice," Kyle said. "He likes children."

"And he has everything you'll need," Mia added.

"Cool," Ryan said. "My dad is going to help me build a maze, and he has a stopwatch I can use. Now I just need to get a CD player and CDs. I want to try letting the mice listen to different kinds of music."

"Don't you already have music you can use?" Mia asked.

Ryan shook his head. "I download all my songs straight to my MP3 player," he said. "And I can't exactly put my headphones on the mice."

"I guess not," Kyle said with a laugh. "Too bad, though. I bet Mrs Lockwood would give you extra credit for teaching mice to wear earphones."

"You can borrow some of my dad's CDs," Mia said. "He mostly listens to music from the '80s. I'm sure he won't mind. And I'll ask my mum if you can use the CD player we keep in the garage."

"Excellent!" Ryan said with a grin. "Thanks!"

"Sometimes my mum plays classical music in her vet clinic at night to help keep the animals calm," Kyle added. "I'm sure she'd be willing to let you borrow one of her CDs, too. I'll ask."

"Okay," Ryan said. "I hope the classical music isn't boring. What if it makes the mice too lazy to run through the maze? But I guess that's the point of the experiment."

A bell chimed as they walked through the front door of Mr J's Pet Haven. Jethro, Mr J's pet parrot, sat on his perch near the front entrance.

"Who's there?" the parrot squawked.

"It's just us, Jethro," Kyle said, pausing by the bird's perch.

Jethro looked at Mia and let out a whistle. "Pretty bird," he squawked.

"I think the parrot has a crush on you, Mia," Ryan said.

"He just wants a treat," Mia said. She grabbed a cracker out of the dish Mr J kept on the counter and fed it to the parrot.

"Mine!" the bird screeched.

"He sounds like my sister!" Ryan said with a laugh.

Just then, Mr J appeared from the back of the store. "Well, if it isn't my favourite customers!" he exclaimed with a grin. "What brings you in today? Anything I can help you find?"

"Our school science fair is next week," Ryan explained. "I need to get some mice for my experiment. I want to find out if music makes them cleverer."

"This sounds like a very interesting project," Mr J said. "You'll have to come back and tell me what happens."

"Definitely!" Ryan said.

Mr J helped Ryan gather the things he'd need. Together, they carried everything to the register. "Let's see," Mr J said. "Water bottles, food, an exercise wheel, bedding, and chew toys. And you'll need to make nesting beds for the mice out of cardboard boxes."

Ryan looked confused. "Nesting beds?" he repeated.

"I'll show you how," Mia offered. "It's easy. You just need a place for them to sleep. We can line it with paper towels or toilet paper so it's soft."

Mr J rubbed his chin. "Now, what are we missing?" he asked.

"The mice!" the children yelled in unison.

"Oh, that's right," Mr J said, shaking his head. "It'd be hard to do your experiment without those!"

He led them to a row of cages filled with mice. There were grey mice and black mice and white mice. There were even spotted mice.

"I don't want white ones," Ryan said. "I won't be able to tell them apart!"

"I don't think you want those ones either," Mia said, pointing to a black mouse and a brown mouse that shared a cage.

"Why not?" Ryan asked.

"Because the brown one is a total bully,"
Mia said.

As they watched, the black mouse took a
chew stick into a corner. As soon as it left, the
brown mouse dragged the chew stick right
back to the middle of the cage. Then the black
mouse picked up the same chew stick and
dragged it back to the corner. They repeated
the routine over and over again.

Kyle peered into the next cage. "This grey
one is hilarious," he said.

Inside the cage, a small, grey mouse ran like
crazy on a plastic wheel. Suddenly, it stopped
running. The wheel lurched, and the mouse
fell out. It got right back up and started
running again.

"I think I should get three mice that are as alike as possible," Ryan said. "That way my experiment will be more accurate."

"I have three mice that are brothers," Mr J said. He moved to a cage that held three black-and-white mice.

"Perfect!" Ryan said, peering at the mice. One had a black spot on its back, one had a black spot on its head, and one was almost entirely black except for a white spot on its middle. "They all have different markings so I'll be able to tell them apart."

Mr J. put the mice into a box and took them to the front of the shop. Ryan paid for his purchases, and the children gathered up the mice and the rest of the supplies.

"Get lost!" Jethro shouted as they left.

"Do you guys want to come inside and help me set up?" Ryan asked when they reached his house.

"Okay," Kyle agreed. "My dad is taking me to the shop later to buy bats for my experiment, but I have time."

Mia and Kyle followed Ryan into his room. Right away, they got to work setting up the cage. Kyle filled the water bottle and attached it to the inside of the cage. Then he spread the bedding around and added the chew toys and food.

When the cage was ready, Mia handed Ryan the box with the mice so he could put them in their cage. "Here you go!" she said.

Ryan immediately handed the box back to her. "Um, that's okay. You can do it," he said quickly. "I . . . uh . . . I have to go to the toilet."

With that, he abruptly hurried out of the room and slammed the door.

What's the problem?

Ryan sat with Kyle and Mia during lunch the next day.

"How are the mice doing?" Kyle asked.

"Fine," Ryan said. "They're eating and drinking and using the wheel. But I don't think they like the orange pieces in their food. They keep dropping them outside the cage."

"What did you name them?" Mia asked.

"Classical, Heavy Metal and Mouse," Ryan said. "That way I can keep track of which one is which during the experiment. Mouse is the one that won't listen to any music."

"Are you going to change their names afterwards?" Kyle asked. "My mum always says that pets should have real names that fit their personalities."

"I bet we could come up with some good ones," Ryan said. "They do some really weird stuff."

"Like what?" Mia asked.

"They're just really hyper," Ryan said. "Classical likes to run in and out of a toilet-paper roll, and Mouse wiggles and squeaks when I put food in the dish."

"That's cute," Mia said.

"I guess so," Ryan said. "Heavy Metal is eating the house I made out of an empty cereal box. It's going to be gone before I can eat enough cereal to make him another one. You should come and see them after school."

"I want to, but I haven't finished my experiment yet," Kyle said.

"Me neither," Mia said. "I set up my bean seeds last night. I'm going to see if they'll grow using anything other than water. I just hope they sprout in time. The science fair is next week!"

"I hope my mice can learn the maze by then," Ryan said.

"Did you start training them?" Kyle asked.

Ryan shook his head. "No, the maze won't be done until tomorrow. You should see it. It's really cool."

"I can stop by tomorrow," Kyle offered.

"Oh. Okay." Ryan looked disappointed. He turned to Mia. "Did you ask your mum about the CD player?"

Mia nodded. "Yeah. She said you could borrow it."

"Great, thanks," Ryan said. "Can you bring it over today with the CD from your dad?"

"Why do you need it today?" Mia asked. "Don't the mice have to learn the maze before they listen to the music?"

"Yeah, but . . ." Ryan thought for a second. "My mum is baking chocolate chip cookies today."

Mia's face immediately brightened. "I love chocolate chip cookies!" she exclaimed. "Save me one, okay?"

"Okay, great, " Ryan said, letting out a sigh of relief.

Ryan called right after Kyle got home from school that afternoon.

"I think there's something wrong with Heavy Metal," Ryan said, sounding nervous. "He's lying on his back, and his legs keep twitching."

"He's probably just sleeping," Kyle said. "Mice take naps during the day and play at night."

"I know you're busy, but can you come over to check?" Ryan asked. "I'm really worried."

Kyle sighed. He really needed to work on his own experiment. Otherwise it'd never get done. But Ryan seemed upset. "I'll be right there," he said.

As soon as Ryan hung up, Kyle called Mia. "I'm pretty sure everything is fine with the mouse," he said, "but Ryan seems really worried."

Mia hurried next door to Kyle's house and they headed to Ryan's together.

"Have you decided how to do your experiment?" Mia asked as they walked.

Kyle nodded. "I need to find a really good hitter, someone who's an average hitter, and somebody who's not very good," he said. "Then I'll get them all to hit with a wooden bat and a metal bat and measure how far the ball goes. Do they make super-long measuring tapes?"

"I don't know," Mia said. "Why don't you use the American football field at school? It already has ten-yard lines marked off."

"That's a great idea!" Kyle said with a grin.

When they got to Ryan's house, his mum let them in and sent them to Ryan's room. Ryan was sitting at his desk, staring into the mouse cage. All three mice were awake and busy.

"They look fine to me," Kyle said.

"They are," Ryan admitted, looking a little embarrassed.

"So what's the problem?" Mia asked.

Ryan sighed. "I'm afraid to pick them up," he said quietly.

4

Mouse on the run

Mia's mouth fell open. "You're afraid of mice?" she asked. "Why?"

"Not really afraid," Ryan said. "It's just that they're so tiny! I don't want to squash them."

"We can fix that," Kyle said. "Maybe if we help you play with them it'll help."

"I hope so," Ryan said. "I have to move them a lot for my experiment."

Kyle opened the cage, and the mouse with a black spot on its head scurried into a corner. Kyle reached in and trapped it under his cupped hand. "Which one is this?" he asked.

"That's Classical," Ryan told him.

Kyle carefully slipped his other hand under the mouse and lifted it out of the cage. He sat on the bed with the mouse trapped in his hands. Classical squirmed around inside.

"Is he trying to get away?" Ryan asked.

"No," Kyle said. "He's sniffing my hand." After a moment, Kyle moved his thumb. The mouse could look out, but he couldn't escape.

Mia captured the mouse with the big, black splotch on its back.

"That's Mouse," Ryan said.

"Hi, little one!" Mia said. She held Mouse up to her cheek and giggled. "His nose tickles!"

"Your turn, Ryan," Kyle said.

Ryan peered into the cage. Only Heavy Metal, the black mouse with the white spot, remained in the cage. He sat up and stared at Ryan. Kyle could almost hear the mouse thinking, *Bet you can't catch me!*

Ryan took a deep breath and reached into the cage. The mouse scampered away twice from his cupped hands before Ryan finally managed to catch him.

Ryan sat down cross-legged between Kyle and Mia, holding the mouse in his hands.

"What if he bites?" Ryan asked. He looked really worried.

"He won't," Mia reassured him. "Don't worry. Mice are really friendly animals. They don't bite people unless they're afraid for their lives."

"He's scratching my hand!" Ryan exclaimed. He instantly let go of the mouse. "Oops!"

Heavy Metal dropped onto the bed. He sat up, wiggled his nose and then ran up the inside of Ryan's trouser leg.

"Ahh! Ahh!" Ryan squealed and shook his leg.

"Don't move!" Mia ordered. "You might hurt him!"

"I can't help it! All those little mouse feet feel really creepy!" Ryan stopped moving and gritted his teeth. "He's sniffing out a good spot to nibble!"

"He's looking for a way out," Kyle said. "Sit still."

Ryan stiffened and squeezed his eyes shut. A minute later, Heavy Metal crawled out of his trouser leg. Ryan laughed and picked him up.

"You're a bad mouse," Ryan said. He sounded stern, but he was grinning. And he was holding the mouse with no problem.

"That wasn't so bad," Ryan said as they put the mice back in the cage. "Maybe my experiment will be okay after all!"

"Where's the maze?" Kyle asked.

"It's in the garage," Ryan said. "We'll move it into my room when it's finished. Do you want to see it?"

Kyle nodded. "Definitely!" he said.

Ryan led them to the garage and showed off the wooden maze he and his dad had built. Only one path went from the starting point to the treat cup at the end. There were several dead ends.

"The glue is still drying," Ryan said, "but it will be ready to go tomorrow."

"What treat are you using?" Mia asked.

"Honey bread," Ryan said. "Or maybe peanut butter. I haven't decided yet."

They were suddenly interrupted by a scream from inside the house. "Eeeeek!" a shrill voice shrieked. "There's a mouse in my room!"

"Uh-oh!" Ryan exclaimed.

"Is that your sister?" Mia asked.

Ryan nodded. "Yeah, that's Megan. And she doesn't sound happy."

"The cage was latched," Kyle said as they ran into the house. "I closed it myself."

"Maybe it's a wild mouse," Ryan suggested hopefully.

"Go away, mouse!" Megan screamed. "Get it out of here!"

They quickly checked the cage in Ryan's room. Heavy Metal was gone.

"I guess he had a little taste of freedom and wanted more," Kyle said.

Megan screamed again. "The little monster is eating my favourite shirt!"

"Coming!" Ryan shouted.

Kyle, Mia and Ryan dashed out the door into the hall. A big, yellow cat ran into Megan's room ahead of them.

"Don't you dare eat my mouse, Tiggy!" Ryan yelled.

Megan was standing on her bed, jumping up and down and looking terrified. "Where is it?" she yelled. "Can it climb up here? I know you did this on purpose, Ryan!"

"No, I didn't!" Ryan protested.

Kyle saw a red jumper on the floor. The mouse ran through the sleeve, out the cuff and dashed under the bed. The cat pounced.

"Tiggy, no!" Ryan shouted.

Mia quickly grabbed the cat and held it at arm's length so she wouldn't get scratched. "Heavy Metal is not a cat snack!" she scolded it.

The mouse suddenly dashed out from under the bed and ran under the wardrobe.

"Get it!" Megan shrieked. "Get it!"

Kyle picked up the jumper and knelt down. "Block that side, Ryan!"

"What if he runs towards me?" Ryan asked, sounding scared.

"Catch him!" Kyle said.

But Heavy Metal was either too tired or too scared to run. When Kyle pushed the jumper under the wardrobe, the mouse ran into the sleeve to hide. Kyle carefully picked the jumper up and carried the mouse back to Ryan's room.

"See, the cage door is still latched," Kyle said. He opened it and put the mouse back inside.

"Then how did he manage to get out?" Ryan asked.

"Through here," Mia said. She pointed at a corner of the cage. One of the wires was bent. Heavy Metal was already trying to wiggle through the opening again.

Ryan bent the wire back into place. "I'd better keep my bedroom door closed from now on," he said. "Just in case."

"Good idea," Kyle said. "Your sister is scary when she freaks out!"

5

Peanut-butter bread and a missing batter

Ryan called Kyle again after dinner on Saturday. "I'm about to start my experiment," he said. "Do you and Mia want to come and watch?"

Kyle had spent the whole day working on his own experiment. He was ready for a break.

"Definitely. I'll be right there," Kyle said. Then he called Mia. She wanted to go, too.

"How's your experiment going?" Kyle asked as they walked down the street towards Ryan's house.

Mia sighed. "Plants are pretty," she said. "But they don't do anything."

"They haven't sprouted yet, huh?" Kyle asked.

"Only one," Mia said with a discouraged sigh.

The maze was set up on a folding table in Ryan's room when Mia and Kyle walked in. Ryan was already set up to give Kyle and Mia a demonstration. He put a piece of bread with peanut butter in the treat cup. Then he placed Classical at the starting point.

"The first time I tried to get them to run through the maze, none of them did anything," Ryan said. "They all just sat there looking confused."

Ryan picked up the treat and let Classical sniff it. Then he moved the bread through the maze, keeping it just out of reach as the mouse followed. "But once they realize there's a good reason to go into the maze in the first place, they all catch on pretty quick," he said.

At the end of the maze, Ryan let the mouse have a little piece of the bread. "This time, I'll use my stopwatch and see how long it takes him," he said. "I want to time them without the music first so I can see if it makes a difference."

When Ryan put Classical down to run the maze again, the mouse took off running. He hit a couple of dead ends and bumped into a wall, but he made it through.

"Thanks for letting us watch," Mia said when they were done. "Mice are way more fun to work with than plants."

"Thank you for the crash course in mouse management," Ryan said. "Now I just have to teach the other two how to run the course. And then I can do my experiment."

On Monday morning, Ryan caught up with Kyle and Mia on their way to school.

"How's the mouse project going?" Kyle asked.

"Great!" Ryan said. "I'm going to start playing music for Classical and Heavy Metal tomorrow. Then I'll see if it changes how fast they go through the maze."

"I'm glad somebody's experiment is working," Mia said, looking frustrated. "Mine certainly isn't."

"Really?" Kyle asked.

"What's wrong?" Ryan asked.

"I've only had one plant sprout," Mia explained. "And it's puny."

"I can't even do my experiment," Kyle complained. "I'm one batter short."

"Getting a baseball player should be easy," Ryan pointed out.

"It is," Kyle said. "Unless you're looking for a bad hitter. No one wants to admit that they're not very good. So I don't have a bad batter for my experiment."

"I'll do it," Ryan said. "I'm the worst batter ever. Besides, I owe you one."

6

Batters up and see how they run

After school, Kyle and Mia walked to the American football field. Mia was going to take a video of Kyle's experiment.

They decided to bring Rex, Kyle's dog, along, too, since he was the best fielder in the county. The only thing the yellow Lab liked more than chasing balls and squirrels was playing with Kyle.

Ryan was already waiting for them at the field when they arrived. Connor Moss and Billy Evans were standing with him. They were both on the school baseball team, and Connor was the best batter in the whole year.

"Thanks for helping me out, guys," Kyle told them.

"No problem," Billy said. "Maybe your experiment will help me hit a home run."

"Maybe it'll help me hit at all. I usually strike out," Ryan said. "Your pitching arm might give out before I hit one, Kyle."

"You'll be okay," Kyle said. "Besides, it's just an experiment, not a game."

Rex sat down and barked.

"I think Rex is ready," Kyle said. "Let's get started!"

Connor clobbered the first pitch with a wooden bat. The ball sailed down the length of the field. Rex chased it down and brought the ball back to Kyle.

The results were similar for Connor's next few hits with the wooden bat, too. But when he switched to the aluminium bat, the ball went so far that it sailed over the fence at the far end of the field.

Rex went nuts. He jumped in the air, but he couldn't get over the fence. He pawed at the ground, but he couldn't dig under it. He barked like mad until Kyle threw another ball towards him.

Kyle had brought extra balls with him, just in case all Connor's hits ended up going out of the park. When Rex chased a ball, he didn't give up until he caught it – or thought he did.

"Good boy," Kyle said when Rex came back with the second ball.

Kyle didn't need extra balls for Billy. Billy hit pop flies and short drives with the wooden bat. He hit one line drive down the centre of the field with the aluminium bat.

"I'm never going to hit a home run," Billy complained.

"I'm never going to hit a single!" Ryan joked.

When it was his turn at bat, Ryan only hit

one out of every four pitches no matter which bat he used. And most of those hits were foul balls. But Rex didn't mind. He chased after the balls anyway.

"What did you find out?" Mia asked as they walked home.

"Aluminium bats are definitely better," Kyle said. "But even a metal bat can't make a bad hitter better."

Maze daze and
a desperate plea

Everyone got to school early on Friday morning so they'd have time to set up their experiments and presentations.

After Mrs Lockwood took the register, the whole class headed outside. Billy Evans was giving his presentation first, and they'd need plenty of fresh air.

"Stink bombs don't smell as bad outside," Billy told the class. He looked a little upset with that fact. "But they wouldn't let me stink up the school! So if you want a good whiff, you'll have to get closer."

Everyone laughed, and a few of the braver pupils took a couple of cautious steps closer to where Billy stood.

Billy held up what looked like a normal egg. "My question was whether or not I could make a stink bomb out of an egg," he explained to the class.

"What did you come up with for the second step of the experiment?" Mrs Lockwood asked, raising her voice. She hadn't stepped closer. "What was already known?"

"Well, I knew that if you leave eggs out on the worktop they go bad," Billy said. "So I thought I'd really take things up a notch. For the experiment step, I poked a hole in this egg, put foil around it, and let it sit in the sun for a few days."

Billy cracked the egg open, and a horrible smell immediately filled the air. The pupils nearby gagged, covered their noses and jumped back.

"I think I'm going to be sick," Mia whispered to Kyle.

Kyle held his nose and nodded.

"Cool!" Billy exclaimed. "It stinks because these little germ things–"

"Bacteria," the teacher said.

"Right," Billy said. "Bacteria got into the egg and turned the insides into really gross, stinky stuff."

"Hydrogen sulphide," Mrs Lockwood told him.

"And that," Billy concluded, "is why rotten eggs smell so bad! So my theory was right. I can turn an egg into a stink bomb!"

Mrs Lockwood grinned. "That's very scientific, Billy."

"You can make stuff that smells even worse," Billy said. "But my dad wouldn't let me."

"Good!" Mia muttered.

The class headed back inside, and several more pupils gave their presentations after Billy. Then it was Kyle's turn. As he made his way to the front of the room, Kyle saw Ryan grin and flash him a thumbs up. He'd given Kyle permission to show the class his less-than-impressive batting skills.

"I did my experiment on baseball," Kyle explained. He pulled up the video Mia had taken on the classroom computer and pressed play. "I wanted to see if batters could hit better with a wooden bat or a metal bat."

Everyone was impressed with Connor's batting abilities, and they thought Rex was amazing. They cheered when Billy hit the ball a long way, and laughed at Mia's footage of Ryan trying to hit the ball.

Ryan missed again and again. One time, he swung so hard that the bat flew out of his hands. Another time, he ducked so the ball wouldn't hit him.

When Ryan finally did manage to hit one, the ball sailed backwards. Rex almost knocked him down chasing after it!

"So I learnt that an aluminium bat can make most batters hit farther," Kyle said with a laugh, "but it can't help a bad batter hit the ball!"

"But Ryan gets an A for trying," Mrs Lockwood said.

Everyone cheered. Ryan stood up and took a bow.

A few other pupils did their presentations. When Mia's name was called, she turned to Kyle. "My project is a disaster," she whispered. "What am I going to do?"

"Just do your best," Kyle said.

Mia took a deep breath and walked over to the table that held her experiment. There were five small plastic cups filled with soil sitting on top, but only one of them had anything growing in it.

"I'm sorry to report that most of my bean seeds failed their growing experiment," Mia said.

The rest of the class laughed, and Kyle smiled at Mia.

"I put seeds in plastic cups and watered them with different liquids. Milk, vinegar, iced tea, fizzy drink and water," Mia explained. "I found out that bean seeds hate vinegar, fizzy drink and iced tea!" She made a face. "But I can't stand those drinks either."

The other pupils laughed in agreement.

"One of the seeds drank milk like a good little bean baby, but then it got a fungus and died," Mia continued.

She moved over to the only plastic cup with a sprout growing in it – her one success. "But the one I grew in water looks great!" she said. "So I learnt two things: don't mess with Mother Nature, and I do not have a green thumb!"

Everyone clapped when she sat down.

"Ryan, you're up," the teacher announced.

Ryan walked over to the table that held his mice. He had everyone's complete attention.

"My experiment was to see if music made mice cleverer and faster," Ryan said. "I used a maze and two different types of music, classical and heavy metal, to do my test. My theory was that the rock music would make the mice faster, and classical would make them slower."

"First, I trained the mice to run the maze without music," Ryan continued. "That way I could work out how well they ran it on their own. Then I played classical music for one mouse, heavy metal for another, and no music for the last mouse."

Ryan put Mouse into the maze to show everyone how his experiment had turned out. Mouse made his way through the maze at a steady pace, not running into any walls along the way.

Next, Ryan held up a chart he'd made that showed the times for the three different mice. "I timed all the mice with no music to start with," he explained, "and then timed them again with the music. Mouse's time is three seconds better than the day he started. Practice makes perfect!"

Ryan let Mouse eat the peanut-butter bread as a reward. He set Classical in the maze next and turned on the music. Classical ran through so fast everyone gasped.

"I kind of thought he might fall asleep after listening to classical music for three days," Ryan said with a laugh. "I know I would! But I was wrong. Classical runs the maze eight seconds faster with the music than Mouse does without it."

"That's pretty amazing," Mrs Lockwood said.

"So is this!" Ryan said. He put the last mouse, Heavy Metal, into the maze and turned on the music.

The poor little mouse had a horrible time getting through the maze. He made wrong turns and bumped into more walls than he had on the first day. He seemed completely lost!

"Whenever I play the music, Heavy Metal can't remember where to go." Ryan said. "I thought it would make him faster, but it just makes him confused! It turns out my theory was backwards – classical music makes mice cleverer, not rock music like I'd expected."

"I can sympathize," Emma said with a laugh. "All that banging would make it hard for me to think, too!"

"Hey, I'm not a mouse," Connor said. "Leave rock music alone."

After lunch, Mrs Lockwood announced the winners of the science fair. "You all did a great job," she said. "Our third-place ribbon goes to Billy and his stink-bomb experiment."

Billy stepped up and claimed his yellow third-place ribbon.

"Second place goes to Kyle for his baseball-bat experiment," the teacher continued. "And Ryan's mouse experiment is our first-place winner!"

"Congratulations!" Mia called as Ryan stepped forward to collect his first-place ribbon. "First place and you have three new pets now!"

Ryan shook his head. "Actually, I don't," he said to the class. "I can't keep them as pets. We already have a cat, and my sister freaked out after one got loose in her room, so my mum won't let me. I thought she'd change her mind, but she didn't. The mice have to go."

Home is where the cage is

On Sunday afternoon, Ryan came over to Kyle's house. Kyle and Mia were playing with Rex on the front porch.

"What are you doing?" Ryan asked as he walked up.

"Trying to teaching Rex the don't-eat-the-cookie-on-your-nose trick," Kyle said.

He broke a dog biscuit in half and held it out in front of Rex's nose. "Rex, sit," he said firmly. Then he put one piece of biscuit on the dog's nose. "Stay!"

But Rex clearly didn't get the point of the trick. Kyle was supposed to put his hands around the dog's snout so he couldn't eat the treat, but Rex was too fast. He tossed the biscuit up in the air and swallowed it whole. Then he wagged his tail and looked up at Kyle.

Kyle threw up his hands. "Rex, you're supposed to stay!" he said.

Mia picked up the second half of the biscuit and tossed it to the dog. "Catch!" she called.

Rex caught it in his mouth and ate it in one bite. He looked up at Kyle expectantly.

"I don't have any more," Kyle said. He showed the dog his empty hands.

Rex sniffed to make sure. Then he spun around and took off after a squirrel that was digging in the garden.

"Did you find anyone to take the mice?" Kyle asked.

"No, not yet," Ryan said.

"Oh, no!" Kyle said. "I'd take them, but I already have Rex. He's enough work as it is."

"I can't take them, either," Mia said. "My cat destroys toy mice. Imagine what she'd do to real mice."

"Maybe Mr J will take them back," Kyle suggested.

"Good idea!" Ryan said. "Let's go find out."

The children walked over to Mr J's Pet Haven. "Hello!" Jethro said as they walked in.

"Well, hello there, my future zoologists!" Mr J greeted them, grinning widely. "How did your musical mouse experiment go?"

"Great!" Mia said. "Ryan won first place."

"And I found out that classical music makes mice cleverer," Ryan added.

"Or maybe it just calms them down so they can concentrate," Mr J suggested. "Do you need more mouse food?"

Ryan shook his head. "Actually, I have a problem," he said. "My mum won't let me keep the mice."

"We can't find anyone else to take them," Kyle said. "Do you think you could take them back?"

"Oh, I'm sorry, but I'm afraid not," Mr J said, shaking his head. "I just got in some new mice.

Ryan sighed. "Okay," he said. "Thanks anyway."

Monday morning didn't bring any better news. "My mum said the mice have to be gone by this afternoon," Ryan told Kyle and Mia when they got to school.

"We have to do something," Kyle said. After Mrs Lockwood took the register, he raised his hand. "Can I talk to the class for a minute?"

"Of course, Kyle," the teacher said. "Go ahead."

"We have to find a home for Ryan's mice or something awful might happen to them," Kyle said. "Can't one of you take them?"

"I already asked, but my dad doesn't think I'll clean the cage," Connor replied. "He won't take a chance even though I promised. Sorry."

"My mum said mice give people the plague," Billy said. "That sounds cool to me, but she said no."

"That was rats in the Dark Ages," Mia corrected him.

"I think she just doesn't want any mice," Billy said.

"I'd do it, but my brother has a python," Lucy Owens said. "My house is a major mouse danger zone."

Mrs Lockwood stood up. "So it seems that all of you would like to keep the mice, but your parents, or your brother's snake, won't let you. Is that right?" she asked.

"Yes!" the whole class shouted.

"Then there's only one solution to this problem," Mrs Lockwood said. She turned to one of the experiment tables and lifted a cardboard box. Ryan's cage was underneath it, and his three black-and-white mice were inside.

"Our class now has three prize-winning mascots!" the teacher said. "I spoke to Ryan's mum, and she brought them by this morning."

"Hooray!" everyone cheered.

"Since they'll be our classroom pets, should we rename them?" Mrs Lockwood asked. "Does anyone have any suggestions?"

"How about Mozart, Slash and Joe?" Mia suggested.

Everyone agreed that those names seemed like the perfect fit.

AUTHOR BIO

Diana G. Gallagher lives in Florida, USA, with three dogs, eight cats and a cranky parrot. She has written more than 90 books. When she's not writing, Gallagher likes gardening, garage sales and spending time with her grandchildren.

ILLUSTRATOR BIO

Adriana Isabel Juárez Puglisi has been a freelance illustrator and writer for more than twenty years and loves telling stories. She currently lives in Granada, Spain, with her husband, son, daughter, two dogs, a little bird and several fish.

GLOSSARY

announcement (uh-NOUNS-muhnt) — a public or formal notice about something

bacteria (bak-TIHR-ee-uh) — microscopic living things that exist all around you and inside you; bacteria can be useful, but some cause disease

concentrate (KON-suhn-trate) — to focus your thoughts and attention on something

experiment (ek-SPER-uh-ment) — a scientific test to try out a theory or to see the effect of something

hypothesis (hye-POTH-uh-siss) — a temporary prediction that can be tested about how a scientific experiment will turn out

participate (par-TISS-uh-pate) — to join with others in an activity or event

FACTS ABOUT MICE

- Mice usually live for one to three years.

- Mice measure about 9 centimetres long and weigh between 14 and 28 grams.

- Mice are rodents. That means they are mammals with sharp front teeth that never stop growing.

- Mice are nocturnal animals, which means they are very active at night but spend most of the day sleeping.

- Mice have tails that are as long as their bodies.

CARING FOR YOUR MOUSE

- Mice don't like cold or sunlight, so place your mouse's cage in a spot that is protected from cold air and sun.

- Mice need friends! It's a good idea to keep two females together, rather than two males, since males tend to fight.

- Clean your mouse's cage at least once a week. Make sure you wash it out and put in fresh bedding.

- It's important to make sure your mouse always has fresh food and clean water. You should check your mouse's food and water supply every day.

DISCUSSION QUESTIONS

1. Were you surprised by the results of Ryan's science fair experiment? Talk about what you expected to happen.

2. What type of music makes it easiest for you to think? Talk about your favourite type of music.

3. Imagine you're in Mia and Kyle's class. Talk about what you would have named the mice if they were your new class pets.

WRITING PROMPTS

1. Imagine you're in Kyle and Mia's class. Write a paragraph about what you would have done for your science fair experiment.

2. Write a paragraph about what type of pet you would like to have. If you already have a pet, write about why you chose your pet.

3. Do you think mice would make good pets? Why or why not? Write a paragraph about your opinion.